Just George

The favourite character from
Enid Blyton's
Famous Five

George, Timmy and the Secret in the Cellar

Just George

The favourite character from

Enid Blyton's

Famous Five

George, Timmy and the Secret in the Cellar

Sue Welford

Illustrated by Lesley Harker

Hodder
Children's
Books

A division of Hodder Headline Limited

First published in Great Britain in 2000
by Hodder Children's Books

10 9 8 7 6 5 4 3 2 1

For further information on Enid Blyton,
please contact www.blyton.com

A Catalogue record for this book is available from
the British Library

ISBN 0 340 77876 8

Typeset by Avon Dataset Ltd, Bidford-on-Avon, Warks

Printed and bound in Great Britain by
The Guernsey Press Co. Ltd, Channel Isles

Hodder Children's Books
a division of Hodder Headline Ltd
338 Euston Road
London NW1 3BH

Contents

Contents

1

Banished!

'It's no good you arguing, Georgina!' said her father loudly. 'That dog has got to stay outside for good!'

'But Timmy didn't *mean* to chew your briefcase,' insisted George. Her vivid blue eyes were blazing angrily. For one thing, her father had called her by her full name, Georgina, when he knew she hated it and for another, the thought of her puppy, Timothy, being banished to the garden filled her with horror.

'I don't care whether he meant to or not,' said her father, a tall, stern-looking man with dark eyebrows which met together in a fierce frown when he was annoyed. 'The fact is that my best leather briefcase is ruined and if that puppy isn't kept outside then you'll have to find him another home!' With that, he stormed off to his study at the other end of the house and slammed the door so hard that all the old windows and doors of the house shook.

There was no doubt about it, poor old Timothy was in trouble again.

'It's not fair,' said George stamping her foot and shaking her head so that her short, dark curls bounced around her head. 'Is it, Timmy darling?'

'Wuff,' said Timothy, a shaggy, brown mongrel puppy who always knew exactly what George was saying to him. He had kept very quiet all the time her father was shouting. Since George had found him on the moor behind her

house and had been allowed to keep him, he had been the happiest dog in the world. The tall man who frowned and whose name was Father said he could stay, *if* he behaved himself. He did try very hard indeed but sometimes he simply couldn't *help* chewing things. It was a puppy's nature. When he saw the strange-looking leather object lying on the chair in the hall he hadn't known it was important. It had just looked very chewable . . .

Timothy looked up at his small mistress with his melting brown eyes. 'Wuff,' he said again, thumping his plumy tail gently on the floor. 'Wuff.'

George bent down to give him a great big hug. Timothy was her best friend and she loved him more than anything else in the world – even if he *didn't* seem to be able to help upsetting her father.

It wasn't difficult to upset George's father. He was a famous scientist and spent many hours in his study doing important work, so hated anyone making a noise and disturbing him. But most of all he hated his things getting chewed!

'Come on, Tim,' said George, sighing. 'Let's go for a walk. By supper time Father will have forgotten you're banished, I'm sure.'

Her father was terribly absent-minded and often forgot what day of the week it was.

George skipped out of the house and down through the garden. It was a bright, fresh, seaside morning. Clumps of flowers nodded their heads in the breeze as the little girl and her puppy passed by.

The house where George lived was called Kirrin Cottage, even though it was really too big to be a proper cottage. It had old whitewashed stone walls and an ancient wooden front door. Roses grew up the walls almost as high as George's little bedroom under the eaves where one window looked out over Kirrin Bay.

The cottage garden was crammed full of flowers and vegetables. George's mother's family had lived in the area for many years and neither George nor her parents could imagine living anywhere else.

George was no ordinary little girl. More than

5

anything she wanted to be a boy. She could run and sail and swim and whistle just as good as any boy you could meet. She had even cut off her hair so she would *look* like a boy as well as acting like one. She had a freckled, snub nose and was as brown as a hazelnut from playing out of doors.

George *loved* living at Kirrin Cottage. The house was set on top of a lovely low cliff overlooking sandy Kirrin Bay. A wonderful little island had guarded the entrance to the rocky bay for hundreds of years. In the centre was a ruined castle with two tumbledown towers that stood proud and mysterious against the sky.

The island had belonged to George's mother for many years and she had promised that one day she would give it to George for her very own.

So, down the garden and out of the gate George and Timothy went on their walk. George tried to forget her quarrel with her father. She put her hands in the pockets of her shorts and whistled a merry little tune.

Whistling always made her feel a million times better.

The two ambled along the narrow path that led straight out on to the moor behind Kirrin Cottage. In one direction it led down to the bay. In another it led to the village. Yet another path went down the lane then across the common towards Kirrin Farm. George's mother had lived there as a child but for some time an old couple, Mr and Mrs Sanders, had been in residence. George loved to visit them and their animals and had promised Timothy she would take him there very soon.

Today, though, the little tomboy decided to walk to the village. On the way she had to pass Kirrin Harbour and she wanted to see her friend Alf. Alf was the son of one of the fishermen. He was very fond of Timothy and the little dog hadn't had a pat and a tit-bit from him for ages.

Timothy scampered on ahead as the two made their way along the track towards the village. It was a lovely day. The sun was shining and skylarks sang. The sky was blue with little cotton-wool clouds rambling across it.

George stopped whistling and took a deep breath of sea air. It really was too nice a day to feel angry for very long. Surely Father would soon forget his threat and let Timothy come back into the house? The puppy had been banished several times before but by the next day Father had usually forgotten.

There was nothing for George to do but keep her fingers crossed!

'Oh, look, Timmy,' cried the little girl as a crimson-and-black butterfly settled on the scratchy heather beside the path. She crouched down. 'Come and see!'

Timothy scampered back towards her. 'Wuff,' he said, cocking up his big ears and eyeing the insect's huge wings. Each one had a bright spot on that looked like an eye staring at him. He tilted his head to one side, then jumped backwards with a little startled whine. He wasn't at all sure he liked the two big eyes gazing at him.

'Silly old Tim,' laughed George, hugging him. 'It won't hurt you.'

Timothy crept closer, sniffing the butterfly. Then he jumped back again as it took off in a flutter of bright wings and flew up and away into the sky.

'Silly boy!' chuckled George again, getting to her feet. 'Come on, I'll race you!'

The two soon came to the edge of Kirrin harbour, where the path ended. They hopped down the bank and ran across the shingle to where the fishing boats were moored. There were six of them, all brightly painted with little square wheelhouses on their decks. Their tall masts tinkled a tune in the sea breeze.

Higher up on the beach were the big, iron winches used to haul the boats out of the sea to rest close to the harbour wall above the tide line until they were ready to sail again.

Alf's father owned a boat called the *Sally Ann*. George's grandfather had given it to Alf's grandad years ago as a reward for saving his life at sea during a storm.

Suddenly George stopped with her hands on her hips and a puzzled frown on her face. Everything was strangely quiet. There were usually lots of fishermen about oiling the winches, mending nets, swabbing down the decks or getting ready to sail out to the Kirrin fishing grounds with the next high tide. She loved watching them as they went about their daily tasks and often sat and chatted to Alf while he was mending his father's fishing nets.

Today, though, the beach and the little harbour were deserted. All George could hear was the swishing of the waves and the cries of the seagulls overhead.

It was very odd indeed.

'Where *has* everybody gone, Timmy?' asked the puzzled little girl.

'Wuff, wuff,' said Timothy sounding rather puzzled too. He had been looking forward to seeing his friend Alf and now there was no-one about. What on earth had happened to everyone? If they didn't turn up soon it looked as though he wouldn't get a tit-bit after all!

2

Bad news

George and Timothy stayed on the beach for a while waiting for Alf to appear. As they walked along the water's edge George found a piece of driftwood and threw it for Timothy.

'Fetch!' she cried, throwing the old piece of wood into the water.

The puppy scrambled down the bank of

shingle and went *splash* into the sea. He couldn't quite swim yet but loved prancing around at the edge of the waves. In fact it was one of his favourite games.

'Wurf, wurf!' he barked loudly at the driftwood bobbing about just out of his reach.

'Fetch it then, Timmy!' shouted George, jumping up and down and shouting at the top of her voice. 'Don't be a scaredy-cat!'

As soon as a wave carried the stick within his reach, Timothy pounced. He turned and came running back proudly with the wood in his mouth.

'Well done! Oh Timmy, you're so brave! Now I'm all wet,' cried George, laughing as Timothy shook himself all over her.

They played for a while longer, then George sat down in the shade of the *Sally Ann*. 'Come and sit down, Timmy. I'm tired out,' she said, stroking the puppy's shaggy head as he sat down beside her. His red tongue was lolling out and he was panting like a steam train. 'Oh dear,' said George, feeling rather annoyed that her friend, Alf, wasn't there to chat to. 'Where *has* everybody gone? We can't wait all day!'

Suddenly Timothy gave a low growl deep in his throat and George noticed a man in a dark suit coming across the beach towards the *Sally Ann*. She knew most of the people who lived in Kirrin but she'd never seen this man before.

The man stopped and stared up at the deck with a frown on his face. Then he walked round to the other side.

George heard him call out: 'I say, is anyone up there?'

George put her hand on Timothy's collar to stop him lunging forward and running to bark at the man. The fur on the back of his neck was standing on end and she could tell he didn't like the look of this stranger.

'Do you know where the fisherman who runs this boat is, young man?' the stranger asked George when he spotted her sitting there.

'I don't know, sorry,' said George, grinning because he had mistaken her for a boy. She was always pleased when people did that. 'We're looking for him as well. Everyone seems to have disappeared this morning. I can't think where they've got to.'

'Well, I'm sure they'll be back soon,' said the man. 'I think I'll wait here.' He walked back to the harbour wall and sat down. George saw him glance at his watch and tap his fingers on his briefcase rather impatiently.

'Come on, Timmy,' said George getting to her feet at last. She felt rather bored with waiting. 'Let's go and buy an ice-cream, shall we? If we can't find Alf we'll have to think of something else to do this morning.'

'Wurf,' said Timothy, eagerly bounding on ahead. One of his favourite treats of all was ice-cream. He liked it even better than tit-bits from his friend Alf.

The puppy scampered along as George ran back up to the sea wall. She hopped over, then stopped at the roadside kerb. 'Sit,' she commanded sternly and Timothy sat obediently beside her.

George knew she must be careful. The village of Kirrin was very sleepy and quiet but cars did come along the street sometimes. 'Good boy,' she said when she had made sure the road was clear. 'Off we go again!'

But the two didn't get as far as the ice-cream shop, for as they passed the little seaside café they spotted rather a strange thing. All the Kirrin fishermen were inside sitting round a table, talking and looking very serious indeed.

'I wonder why they're all in there?' said George, peering in.

'Wurf,' said Timothy as if to say, *'Let's go in and find out, shall we?'*

Through the window George saw that Alf

was there with his father. Father and son were like two peas in a pod. They both had a shock of dark brown hair and their faces were ruddy and tanned from the sunshine and the salty sea air.

'Come on, Timmy,' said George when she spotted her friend. 'Let's go and say hello.'

Alf looked surprised when George and Timothy came through the door.

'Hello, George. Hello, Timmy old boy,' he said, bending to stroke Timothy as the little dog jumped up at him. 'What are you two doing here?'

'We've come to say hello,' explained George. 'We've been waiting down at the harbour. We haven't seen you for ages and Timmy was dying for one of your tit-bits.'

'Well, I'd better see what I can find, then,' Alf said, fishing in his pocket and coming up with rather a grubby-looking peppermint. 'There you are, old boy, will that do?'

'Wurf,' said Timothy gobbling the sweet up in no time at all and looking up hopefully for more.

'Sorry,' said the boy giving them a lop-sided grin. 'That's all I've got today.' He turned his pockets inside out but there were only bits of string, a penknife, a handkerchief smelling of fish and a box of matches. No more peppermints at all!

'Wuff,' said Timothy lying down at Alf's feet. After all, one peppermint was better than none! He put his nose on his paws and gave a sigh.

Alf had been George's friend for a long time. He was older than she was and had left school to work on his father's boat. The two earned their living fishing the waters of Kirrin Bay. They lived in one of the little white painted fishermen's cottages along by the harbour.

Alf's father and the other fishermen were talking in loud voices.

'I don't see how we can prove it,' said Alf's father putting his head into his hands. 'It looks as if I'm going to lose the *Sally Ann*. I don't know what my son and I are going to do if we can't earn our living! We might have to move to the town to find work.'

George couldn't help overhearing. 'Lose the

19

Sally Ann!' she exclaimed in a horrified voice. 'What on earth does your father mean, Alf?'

Alf pulled a very wry face indeed. 'Dad's had a letter from the ministry,' he explained.

'What's a ministry?' asked George with a frown.

'It's a government department that looks after the fishing industry,' continued Alf. 'The letter said someone has written to them saying my dad doesn't own the *Sally Ann*.'

'Who wrote such a silly letter?' asked George indignantly. 'Of *course* he owns the *Sally Ann*.'

'They won't tell us who wrote it,' said Alf sadly. 'But they believe what it says and we might have to give up the boat.'

'Well, it's perfectly stupid,' said George, feeling more and more angry. '*My* grandad gave the *Sally Ann* to *your* grandad.' Her mother had often told her how Alf's grandfather had bravely rescued her father. George had always thought the story very exciting and wished she could have been there when it happened.

'I know,' said her friend sadly. 'But we haven't got any papers to prove it.'

'Mummy can prove it!' insisted George, now feeling very angry indeed. How could anyone write such a letter telling such awful lies. '*She* can tell the ministry.'

'That's just it, Master George,' said Alf's father, overhearing. He knew she hated being called by her full name and always called her *Master* George with a twinkle in his eye. '*We* can insist your grandfather gave us the boat, but we haven't got any legal papers to prove it.'

'And you see, George,' said Alf. 'Fishermen aren't allowed to fish in Kirrin waters unless they own their own boat. So it looks as if me and my dad are out of a job!'

3

Trouble!

When the fishermen had finished their meeting, George and Timmy went back down to the beach with them. George felt very worried about Alf and his father losing their boat and couldn't help feeling sad as she walked along beside him. Things just wouldn't be the same if he had to move away from Kirrin. Even though

Timothy was her best friend, Alf was her friend too and she would miss him very much indeed.

She suddenly remembered someone had been looking for Alf's father.

'There was a man looking for you earlier,' she said, running to catch up with him as he strode on ahead.

The burly fisherman frowned. 'A man? What did he want?'

'I don't know,' said George. 'But he said he would wait until you came back.'

Alf's father hurried across the road to where the man was waiting. He was still sitting on the harbour wall looking rather hot and bothered in his smart suit on such a sunny day. He stood up when he saw the fisherman hurrying towards him.

The others caught up and stood watching Alf's father and the stranger talking to one another. Alf's father was looking grim.

'I've come to check that you received our letter about ownership of the *Sally Ann*,' George heard the man say. 'You haven't replied to it yet.'

'No, but I can tell you now,' said Alf's father angrily. 'That boat is mine, fair and square.' He looked very upset. 'And you can't prove otherwise!'

'He's from the ministry,' said Alf gloomily. 'He's telling Dad he's got to give up the boat.'

'He can't do that!' exclaimed George scowling. 'I'm going to tell him the *Sally Ann* belongs to you!'

The small girl strode across the shingle looking very determined and fierce. Timothy scampered after her. When his mistress looked like that he knew there were going to be fireworks!

'I've come to tell you my grandfather gave the *Sally Ann* to Alf's grandad,' said George to the man, her eyes blazing fiercely. 'So you can't take her away from him!'

'I'm sorry, son,' said the man from the ministry. 'But if no-one can prove the ownership of the boat then the fishing licence will be taken away.' He turned to Alf and his father looking very stern. 'You've got five days to find written proof of your ownership. Good

day to you all!' With that he turned on his heel and strode away across the beach.

Everyone stood and stared, feeling stunned. Alf's father frowned angrily as the other fishermen, who had just arrived back in time to see the man striding off, gathered around him, all talking at once.

Alf went to join the huddle of men. They were all shaking their heads and talking amongst themselves. There was no doubt about it. Things looked very grim indeed for Alf and his poor father.

They seemed to have forgotten George was there. 'Come on, Timmy,' she said, sighing sadly. She wished with all her heart there was something she could do to help. 'We'd better get back to see if Father's got over his bad mood and will let you back indoors.'

'Wuff,' said Timothy scampering on ahead. He didn't really understand what had happened but he could tell that George's father wasn't the only human in a bad temper that day!

George walked along the narrow path with

Timothy scampering on ahead as usual. She felt rather gloomy and glum now. It would be too horrible if her friend Alf and his father weren't allowed to fish in the Kirrin waters any more. It would be even worse if they had to move away. Alf, his father *and* grandfather had lived in the village all their lives. She simply couldn't imagine how horrid it would be to have to move away from Kirrin. It was the very nicest place in the world. If only there was *something* she could do to help!

George decided she would ask her mother. *She* always knew what to do.

'Come on, Timmy,' she said, hurrying. 'The sooner we tell Mummy about this, the sooner we might be able to do something to help.'

When the two reached home, they found Joanna, the kindly woman who helped George's mother in the house, in a bit of a flap.

'We've run out of eggs,' she wailed to George's mother as George and Timothy hurtled in through the door. 'I promised Mr Quentin an omelette for tea. He won't be very pleased to have to make do with something else.'

Quentin was George's father and if someone made a promise to him he expected them to keep it.

'Mummy, I must speak to you about something very important,' said George anxiously.

'I'm sorry, darling,' said her mother, bending to give her a hug. 'I'm just off to catch the train to London and I'll miss it if I don't hurry.'

George's mother was going to spend a few days with George's aunt and uncle.

The aunt and uncle had three children who were George's cousins. Their names were Julian, Dick and Anne. They had never been to Kirrin Cottage so George had never met them. She didn't particularly want to either. Especially as one was a girl! She liked being on her own and hated the thought of other children coming to stay.

'Oh, Mummy, it won't take a minute,' pleaded George.

Her mother glanced at the clock. 'I'll

telephone you this evening,' she said, 'and you can tell me then.'

'And what about my eggs?' wailed Joanna.

'Well, I'm sorry, Joanna,' said George's mother. 'I don't have time to worry about *them* either. Quentin will probably have forgotten he was to have an omelette anyway.'

'Yes, I suppose he might have done,' said Joanna with a sigh. 'But I don't know what else I'm going to give him.'

'Now be a good girl while I'm away, dear,' said George's mother giving her daughter a

hug. 'And don't let Timmy chew anything else of Father's.'

'No, Mummy,' said George, hugging her back.

'And do as Joanna tells you,' her mother added. 'She's going to look after you while I'm gone.'

'Yes, Mummy,' said George again, kissing her mother's cheek. 'Have a nice time in London.'

George's mother picked up her suitcase and went out. 'Bye, dear,' she called. 'I'll see you next week.'

'Oh, blow!' said George when her mother had gone. She plonked herself down at the kitchen table, leaning her chin on her hands. 'Blow, blow! If Mummy can't help Alf I don't know *what* we can do.'

'What on earth do you mean, George, dear?' asked Joanna sitting down beside her. 'What's happened to Alf?'

George quickly explained.

'Oh, dearie me!' exclaimed Joanna when she heard. 'What will they do?'

'I've no idea,' said George with a sigh.

'Well, it's no good you worrying about it,' said Joanna. 'Something will turn up, I expect. It usually does. Now run and play, there's a good girl.'

'We're too fed up to play,' said George gloomily. 'Aren't we, Timmy?'

'Wuff,' said Timothy, lying down and putting his head on George's foot.

But then a smile suddenly spread across Joanna's round, jolly face as an idea came into her head. 'If you haven't got anything to do then *I've* got a job for you.'

'What *kind* of a job?' asked George, warily. Joanna's idea of a job sometimes meant tidying her bedroom and George hated doing that.

'You could go to Kirrin Farm and fetch me some nice fresh farm eggs for your father's tea,' said Joanna. 'And that would solve *my* problem.'

'That *is* a good idea,' said George cheering up a bit. 'I'd promised to take Timmy there. Hear that, Tim? We're off to Kirrin Farm!'

Timothy's ears pricked up at the sound of

the word 'farm'. His little mistress was always talking about the place. Did she mean they were really going there at last?

'We could stop for a picnic on the way,' said George suddenly. 'I know lots of lovely picnic places. That will cheer us up no end, won't it, Timmy?'

'Wurf,' said Timothy, jumping up at her. Picnics were another of his favourite things.

So Joanna packed a picnic for George and her puppy to stop and eat on the way to Kirrin Farm. There were ham sandwiches, rosy red tomatoes, sticks of crisp celery, an apple and a huge slice of fruit cake. All to be washed down with homemade ginger beer, straight from the bottle.

Timothy had some of his special biscuits that took quite a long time to munch through. His nose twitched as he smelled them going into the picnic bag.

'I'll put the bag into this basket,' said Joanna fetching a square wicker basket from the cupboard. 'You can carry the eggs home in it. They'll be nice and safe in there.'

'Come on, Timmy,' called George excitedly when the basket was ready. 'You're off to Kirrin Farm at last!'

4

Quiet as a lamb

Down the lane they went, and on to the stony road that led across the common. It was lovely walking in the sunshine. George strode along, swinging the wicker basket to and fro.

'I feel like Little Red Riding Hood,' she called out to Timothy who was scampering on ahead. His nose was fixed firmly on the ground as he hunted for new and exciting smells. Once he smelled a mouse that had scurried across the road and into the hedge. Then he came across a worm-smell and buried his nose in the grass to try to find it. He began to dig, his sharp claws sending showers of earth into the air.

'Buck up, Timmy!' called his mistress. 'It's too nice a day to go digging!'

Timmy didn't think that it was *ever* too nice to be digging but he scampered after his mistress anyway. He didn't much like to be out of her sight unless there was something *really* thrilling to investigate.

The puppy trotted on ahead, eyeing the rabbits' white tails that bobbed away in all directions. He longed to chase them but knew he wasn't allowed.

After a short while George's stomach began to rumble.

'Picnic time, Timmy,' said the little girl, climbing over a stile that led into a field beside the lane. 'I'm absolutely starving!'

Timothy followed, squeezing under the fence at the side of the stile.

'Here's a good place to sit,' said George making a flat place in the long, warm grass and sitting down. 'Look, you can see right across to the sea.'

'Wuff,' said the puppy, sitting down beside her with his long, pink tongue lolling out. He stopped panting to lick George's hand.

With a wonderful view of the shining sea in the distance, George and Timothy settled in the grass to eat their picnic.

Joanna had put a red and white checked cloth inside the basket. George spread it out on the ground beside her. She laid out the sandwiches, celery and tomatoes beside Timothy's store of special biscuits.

'Now, one at a time, please,' scolded the little girl gently as the puppy tried to gobble up all his biscuits at once. 'If you eat nicely, I'll give you one of my ham sandwiches too.'

'Wurf, *crunch*,' went Timothy.

Soon all George's food had gone. All that was left was an apple core. George sat back in the grass feeling quite full up. 'That was scrumptious, wasn't it, Tim?'

'Wuff,' agreed Timothy whole-heartedly. Joanna's picnics were *always* scrumptious. All around were the murmurs of bees in the grass and the songs of skylarks rising up and down in the warm summer air. Timmy gave a contented little sigh. He really was the luckiest dog in the whole world.

'Come on, then, Tim,' said George getting to her feet at last and picking up the empty basket. 'Let's get to the farm now. I'm sure you'll love all the animals there. *And* old Mr and Mrs Sanders. They're both very nice people.'

'Wuff,' said Timothy agreeing as usual.

Along the path they trotted and up the hill to the farm.

'There it is!' called George, pointing to a white stone farmhouse standing strong and lovely on the hillside. She broke into a trot. 'Come on, Timmy, buck up! Let's see if Mr and Mrs Sanders are at home!'

When they arrived, George hesitated in front of the big wooden farm gate that led into the yard. The farmer had two collie dogs who might not like a new dog coming into their territory.

There was no sign of Ben and Rikky, the farm dogs, so George pushed open the gate and went through.

'Hello, Master George!' came a surprised voice from the dairy. A sprightly old lady wearing a flowery summer dress and black Wellington boots came out carrying a bucket in each hand. 'How nice of you to pay us a visit! We haven't seen you for ages and ages.'

'Hello, Mrs Sanders,' said George, grinning. She loved people calling her Master George, it made her feel as if she really *was* a boy. 'I've come for some eggs and to show you my new puppy.'

'Well, that *is* nice,' said the old lady.

'I wasn't sure if your dogs would mind him coming here, though,' said George.

'Oh, don't you worry about them,' said the farmer's wife. 'They're up on the hill seeing to the sheep with Mr Sanders, but I'm sure they'll love to meet this little fellow.' She bent down to give Timothy a pat on the head.

'I found him,' explained George as Mrs Sanders took them into the big farmhouse kitchen.

'Found him? My, my that *was* a piece of luck,' said Mrs Sanders bustling about. 'Now what will you have to drink on this fine summer's day? Lemonade, ginger beer? And I've just made a batch of biscuits so you'll have to have some of those too.'

'Oh, dear,' laughed George. 'We've just had the most enormous picnic, but I'm sure we can find room for some of your delicious biscuits!'

So George sat at the big farmhouse kitchen table with a glass of lemonade and a biscuit. The biscuit smelled mouth-wateringly good and was still warm from the big old oven that belted out heat even in the middle of summer.

'I'm going to show Timmy all the animals,' said George. 'He's never even seen a cow before.'

'You do that, Master George,' said the farmer's wife. 'I've got to finish cleaning out the dairy then I'm off to market on my bicycle, so I'll leave you to collect as many eggs as you like and show your little friend around the place.'

'Thank you,' said George, finishing her lemonade in one big gulp. 'Come on, Timmy, I'll show you the cows first.'

The black-and-white Friesian cows were out in the field behind the long barn. They came ambling across when they saw George and Timothy looking at them from the gate.

As they got closer, Timothy took a step or two backwards. He was not sure he liked these huge, square animals with big hooves and swishing tails. They smelled funny too. A sort of *farm* smell that he hadn't encountered before.

'It's all right, Timmy,' laughed George. 'They won't hurt you.'

One had come right up to the gate and put its big head down to sniff at the little dog. The cow's huge nostrils flared and its long, rough tongue came out to try to lick him.

'See, Timmy,' said George. 'She likes you.'

Timothy didn't feel afraid any more. He always licked people that *he* liked too.

'You must go and see Billy,' said Mrs Sanders, coming up behind them pushing her bicycle. She had finished the dairy and was just off to market. 'He's in the pen behind the dairy.'

'Billy?' exclaimed George. 'Who's he?'

'Come and see,' said the old lady rather mysteriously. She pushed her old bicycle across the yard with her Wellington boots going clunk, clunk on the rough ground as she walked.

Billy was a bull. A very *large* bull indeed. He snorted as Mrs Sanders and the other two came

towards him. He had a big black face and huge brown eyes with long eyelashes and a ring through his nose. George thought he was wonderful.

'Oh, he's *lovely*,' exclaimed the little girl. 'Is he very fierce?' she asked, climbing up the side of the pen to scratch his wiry head.

'Fierce?' said Mrs Sanders, laughing loudly. 'Goodness me, no. He might *look* fierce with that ring through his nose but he's really as gentle as a lamb.'

'That's good,' said George, giving the enormous animal one last pat on his thick neck. 'Because he's very, very big!'

Timothy had trotted off into the barn. He was rather relieved to leave the huge animal behind. Mrs Sanders said he wasn't fierce but he was the biggest animal Timothy had ever seen in his life and the little dog thought it best to keep out of his way. Besides, he had spotted a big stack of straw bales and had decided they might be rather fun to explore. He eyed the flock of hens scratching and pecking in the yard but didn't think they were worth chasing. The silly looking birds had very short legs and probably wouldn't be able to run very fast.

Timothy's ears pricked up as he stood in the tall barn doorway. He could hear lots of mysterious little snuffles and sniffles coming from under the floor and smell lots of exciting smells.

Very interesting indeed!

5

Where are you, Timmy?

While Timothy was exploring the barn, George said goodbye to Mrs Sanders, then began to collect the eggs for Joanna.

She went back into the farmhouse to fetch the wicker basket and came out with it over her arm.

'I'm collecting the eggs, Timmy,' she called

loudly so her puppy would know what she was doing. He must be having a thrilling game to be away from her for so long.

Soon the little girl had found a dozen lovely brown eggs. Some of them were still warm from being laid.

'Here's some,' she said to herself as she peered under the hedge and found a clutch of three beautiful warm eggs. There were several more in the nest box of the hen loft and a few in a makeshift nest underneath the tractor.

'Mrs Sanders must have a lovely time collecting these every evening,' she thought to herself as she placed the eggs carefully in the basket. When she had enough, she put the basket down and went to find Timothy.

Timothy was having the time of his life. He had discovered that the sniffings and snufflings were rats and he was busy chasing them.

Up and down the straw bales the little puppy went. Poking his nose in between them, scrabbling like mad to push down into the gaps so he could catch those quick, grey creatures. Round and round he circled, bits of straw flying about like snowflakes. He really was having a most thrilling time.

Then Timmy saw what must have been the biggest rat in the world. It sat on a bale looking at him with dark bright eyes, whiskers twitching. Suddenly it gave a squeak and shot off, running along the wall before disappearing down a hole in the very corner of the barn.

Timothy sped off after it. How proud of him his mistress would be if he laid such a huge creature at her feet.

The puppy skidded to a halt beside the hole in the floor. Then, to Timothy's horror, there was a creak and a groan and the rotten boards gave way beneath him. With a little yelp of fright, he fell with a crash into the deep, dark cellar below.

The puppy lay on the floor, stunned for a second or two. Then he got up, shook himself and looked around. The rat had disappeared into the gloom. He gave a little whine. It was rather frightening down here. Hopefully, his mistress would come to find him very soon!

Then the little dog heard George calling him.

'Timmy! Timmy, where are you? I've got the

eggs, it's time we were getting home,' she called from the doorway. Where was that naughty puppy? He must have found something very exciting indeed to be gone for so long!

Then George heard a muffled whine from the far end of the barn.

'Timmy!' called George sternly, striding towards the sound. 'Come out at once!'

She reached the hole in the floor and stared down in dismay. 'Timmy!' she cried in horror when she realised the puppy had fallen through. 'Are you all right? Oh, you poor darling!'

'Wuff,' said Timothy rather sheepishly from below. He tried to jump up but only fell back again, rolling over and over on the dusty floor.

'Don't worry, Timmy, I'll rescue you,' cried George looking round for another way into the cellar. 'There must be a door somewhere.'

She soon spotted it. A trap-door in the floor a little way away from the place where the puppy had fallen through. She ran over and tried to pull it open. It was stuck fast.

George took her penknife from her pocket and opened the blade. She put it between the door and the frame but the blade wasn't strong enough and was in danger of snapping off. 'It's no good, Timmy,' she panted. 'I'll have to look in Mr Sanders' workshop for something to prise it open.'

She ran outside and into the workshop. She soon found just what she was looking for! A big iron crowbar. She lugged it back into the barn and managed to prise the door open wide enough to prop up on an old bucket standing nearby. The gap was just wide enough for her to wriggle through and jump down into the cellar.

'I'm here, Timmy,' she panted as she landed. 'I've come to rescue you.'

It was murky in the cellar and the only light came from the gaps between the floorboards above. George could just make out wooden apple barrels and some old tin trunks and suitcases, a twisted bicycle wheel and old tins of paint. There were piles of old newspapers too. The air smelt dry and brittle with the dust of centuries.

But what George couldn't see was her puppy. He had completely disappeared.

Then George heard a bark from the far end of the barn cellar. Timothy had found some more ratty smells. 'Wuff, wuff,' he called as if to say, 'I'm here.'

'Oh, Timmy!' shouted George, threading her way through piles of old junk towards him. Timothy was crouched down, sniffing at a large crack in the dry, earth floor.

'Honestly, Timmy!' said George giving him a hug. 'You *have* led me a merry dance. I wondered what had happened to you!'

Timothy licked her nose and gave a funny gruff little bark. Then he rolled over for a tummy tickle, gazing up at her with his smiley eyes. He was sorry to have worried his mistress but when a dog spies a rat he just has to chase it – even if it means falling through floorboards!

'This is a very interesting place,' said George, looking round curiously. She gave a sudden sneeze. 'Oh, dear, Tim, all this dust is getting up my nose. Look at all this junk. It must be years and years old.'

'Wuff,' agreed the puppy, rolling back on to his feet and sniffing curiously at an old trunk.

'I wonder what's in there?' asked George. She was a very inquisitive little girl and often couldn't resist poking her nose into things.

She undid the clips and opened the lid. It came up with a groan and a squeak of rusty hinges.

'It's old papers and things, Timmy,' she exclaimed, rummaging through the contents. 'I wonder who they belong to?'

Timothy put his nose in and gave a sniff. There were no rat or mouse smells here.

George drew out a old and yellowed envelope. The address was too faded to make out in the gloom but she could just see that it had a very old stamp on the front which looked rather interesting.

'I wonder if Mrs Sanders would mind if I took this home to show Father?' said George, holding the envelope up in a shaft of light so that she could see it better. 'He's very interested in old stamps.'

Timothy gave a small whine as he sniffed it. He didn't think stamps were very interesting at all and the paper smelled musty and horrid. Not a bit like an exciting rat smell.

He wandered off, sniffing and snuffling and scratching around in his usual nosy manner.

George put the envelope in her pocket. 'I'm sure she *won't* mind,' she said. 'She probably doesn't even know all this old junk is here. No-one's been down here for years by the look of it.'

She made her way back to the trap-door. 'Come on, Timmy!' she called, dragging a square wooden box underneath so Timothy could jump on it and she could help him scramble out.

Timothy scampered towards her and jumped up on the box. George managed to heave him up so he could scramble out through the trap-door. 'You'd make a jolly good circus dog,' George giggled as Timothy's back legs and tail disappeared through the hole.

But as the last bit of the puppy disappeared, there was a clang from above as he knocked the bucket to one side. The trap-door suddenly gave a creak and slammed back down, narrowly missing his tail. Timothy jumped back in alarm with a startled yelp.

'Timmy!' yelled George as the door closed with a thump above her head. 'How did you manage to do that, for goodness sake?' She stood on the box with her hands on her hips, staring upwards. 'How do you expect me to get out now?'

'Wuff,' came Timothy's worried bark from

above. He didn't like the thought of George stuck down in the cellar one little bit.

George put her shoulder to the door and heaved. She was a very strong and determined little girl but she simply couldn't shift it. It seemed to be stuck fast.

'Wuff,' barked Timothy, scrabbling madly at the frame. He sat down with his head on one side and gave a little whine of regret. He wasn't sure quite how this had happened. He hadn't *meant* to knock the bucket aside. It had just been there in front of him as he wriggled out.

'Timmy!' panted George from below. 'I can't open it. What on earth are we going to do?'

Mrs Sanders had gone to the market and Mr Sanders was up on the hill with the sheepdogs. There was no-one around to hear her. No-one at all.

6

Rescue

George sat cross-legged on the floor, racking her brains to try to work out what to do.

Above her head, Timothy was still trying to open the trap-door. He scrabbled and scrabbled but it still wouldn't budge.

'It's no good,' shouted George from below. 'You'll only make your paws sore. You might as well give up.'

But Timothy wasn't the kind of dog who gave up. He was as stubborn as his small mistress when it came to trying to solve problems. He sat down for a moment to think. There *had* to be something he could do.

Down below, George sat on the box with her knees drawn up to her chin. It was very gloomy down here and there were lots of strange scratching noises. She didn't much like the thought of being stuck in a cellar infested with rats. She got up and went to explore, hoping there might be another trapdoor somewhere.

The cellar went the whole length of the barn floor but nowhere could the small girl find another exit. She searched and searched, bumping into old boxes and bits of machinery until her legs felt quite bruised. She was determined not to give up but by the time she got back to where Timothy was waiting above, she felt very angry and impatient.

'It's no good, Tim,' she shouted through the gap in the floorboards. 'We'll just have to jolly well wait until Mr or Mrs Sanders gets back.'

With that she plonked down on the box again with a big sigh. It looked as if Father might not get his omelette for tea after all!

Timothy had given up digging and was lying on top of the trap-door with his nose between his paws. Now and then he gave a sad little whine. He could just see his mistress in the gap between the floorboards. She was looking very fed up indeed!

It seemed a long time later when two big black-and-white sheepdogs suddenly appeared in the doorway and came bounding towards him. They barked and sniffed and wagged their long, feathery tails in the air so fast they were just a blur.

'Ben! Rikky!' boomed a stern voice. A man with a wrinkled face and grey hair under an old flat cap appeared. What *were* those dogs making such a fuss about? It was Mr Sanders and he was surprised to see a small, shaggy brown puppy wagging its tail and making friends with his two farm dogs.

'Well,' said the astonished man, 'what
have we here? Where have *you* come from, little
chap?'

'Wuff!' said Timothy leaving his new friends
and going back to try to open up the trap-door
again. He felt sure if he barked loud enough
and scrabbled hard enough this human would
know George was trapped below.

'What have you found, then, little fellow?'
asked Mr Sanders. 'Is it a rat or a mouse?
There's plenty of those in here, that's for

sure. You ask Ben and Rikky, here.'

'Wuff, wuff,' barked Timothy, madly running to and fro. There was no time to ask his new friends about rats and mice, he wanted George to be rescued.

Down below, George had heard Mr Sanders' heavy footsteps on the floorboards. She heaved a sigh of relief. Surely the old farmer would be able to open the stubborn trap-door?

'Mr Sanders,' called out the little girl. 'I'm trapped down here. Could you get me out, please?'

The farmer frowned and looked around. The voice sounded just like young Master George. Where on earth was it coming from?

'Wurf,' barked Timothy standing on the trap-door. 'Wurf, wurf!'

'Down here!' shouted George. 'I'm stuck!'

'Well, I never,' said Mr Sanders moving Timothy gently aside and trying to heave open the trap-door. 'It *is* Master George. I *thought* it sounded like you. What are you doing down there, young lady?'

'The door slammed shut,' shouted George

scowling. She hated being called 'young lady' and she didn't like being stuck in dusty old cellars very much either.

Mr Sanders tried to heave open the door but it wouldn't move. 'I'll just go into my workshop and get a crowbar,' he called. 'Sit tight, young lady.'

'There's one just there,' called George. 'I had to use it to open the door and rescue Timmy when he fell through the floorboards. *That's* why I'm down here in the first place!'

Mr Sanders soon found the crowbar and levered open the door. It opened right up this time and fell backwards with a loud thump.

George jumped on the box and hoisted herself out. 'Oh, thanks, Mr Sanders! That's a relief, I can tell you!' she said, trying to brush all the dust and cobwebs off her shorts. 'I'm jolly pleased to be out of that spidery place.'

'This is *your* puppy, then, is it?' asked the old man, grinning broadly. He knew young George behaved like a boy but he had never seen her looking quite so dusty and dirty before.

'Yes,' said George proudly, grinning as

Timothy jumped all over her, delighted to see her again.

'My word, he's a clever little chap,' said Mr Sanders admiringly. 'He showed me where you were.'

'He's the cleverest dog in the world,' said George, hugging Timothy. 'Aren't you, Tim?'

'Wurf,' said Timothy. Now that his mistress was safe and sound he ran off to see the farm dogs out in the yard. Hens scattered, squawking, in all directions as the three dogs romped together.

'I'd better get back home now, Mr Sanders,' said George. 'I came for some eggs and to introduce Timmy to all your animals.'

'That's nice,' said the farmer with a grin. 'Come any time, Master George. We're always pleased to see you.'

'Thanks, Mr Sanders,' said George, picking up the egg basket and calling for Timothy. 'And thanks again for rescuing me. Come on, Tim. We'll be back in time for Father's tea after all if we get a move on.' In all the excitement she had completely forgotten about the old

envelope stuffed in her pocket.

Through the farmyard the two went, skipping out into the lane and across the common towards Kirrin Cottage. The two collie dogs stood at the farm gate, watching them go. Timothy turned and gave a loud bark, as if to say, *See you again soon.*

'That was quite an adventure, wasn't it, Tim?' said George as she hurried along. She quickly forgot how spidery and mysterious the cellar had been.

'Wurf,' agreed Timothy, scampering ahead. He had met lots of animals, made two new friends, almost caught a rat and helped to rescue his mistress. It had been a most exciting day indeed!

7

The letter

Joanna was in the kitchen baking a batch of delicious-smelling bread as George and Timothy hurtled in through the back door.

'Oh, lovely, thank you, George,' she said as the little girl plonked the egg basket on the table. 'Did you have a nice time at the farm?' She stared at George's grubby shorts and shirt.

'You've got yourself in a bit of a mess, haven't you?'

'Yes, but we had a jolly super time,' said George recounting their adventures.

'Trapped in the cellar?' said Joanna. 'I don't know, you two! You could have been stuck down there for days, George, dear.'

'Oh no, I wouldn't have been,' said George shaking her head. 'Timmy would have told everyone where I was, wouldn't you, Tim?'

'Wuff,' said Timothy.

'You're just two scallywags, both of you,' said Joanna, laughing. 'Whatever will you get up to next?'

'More adventures, we hope,' giggled George. 'Don't we, Timmy?'

Timmy woofed in agreement. He loved having adventures, especially if they meant sniffing out rats.

The two went out into the garden until it was time for tea.

'Let's go up into the tree house, shall we, Tim?' suggested George. She had built the house up in one of the old apple trees. It was rather untidy and ramshackle but very safe.

George put Timothy into his special harness and hoisted him up. Then she climbed the ladder.

They were sitting looking out over the sea when George suddenly remembered the letter and dragged it from her pocket.

'I wonder why it was never posted?' she said curiously. 'Perhaps whoever wrote it was rather forgetful, like Father.'

'Wurf,' said Timothy sniffing the envelope and then sneezing because it still smelled musty.

As George turned the letter over she noticed the flap had come unstuck. She knew it was rather rude to read other people's letters but this one was so ancient she felt *sure* nobody would mind.

She took it out and unfolded it. The letter *had* been written many years ago, in a strange, old-fashioned hand.

As she read line after line, the little girl's heart began to beat very loudly and quickly indeed. Suddenly she gave an excited shout. The letter

had been written by her grandfather who had once owned Kirrin Farm. It contained some very thrilling news. News that a friend of George's would be very, very pleased to hear!

'Timmy!' she exclaimed, her eyes shining. 'You'll never guess in a hundred years what this letter says!'

'Wurf?' said Timothy, his head on one side. He had been wondering why his mistress was looking so delighted.

'Just wait until I show it to Alf's father!' said George, so thrilled she forgot to explain. 'Quick, let's go and tell Joanna!'

She carefully put the letter back into the envelope. It had suddenly become very important and she knew she must take great care of it.

The little girl's heart was still thumping with excitement as she bundled Timothy into his sling and lowered him carefully to the ground.

She climbed down after him and ran indoors with the puppy scampering at her heels. Timothy felt rather puzzled at George's behaviour. Something very wonderful had happened. What on earth could it be?

'Joanna! Joanna!' called George as she hurtled in through the kitchen door. 'I've found a letter written by my grandfather handing the *Sally Ann* over to Alf's grandad.'

'Don't be silly, dear,' said Joanna, bustling about getting the tea ready, 'your grandfather has been dead for years. How could he have possibly written such a letter?'

'No, I mean I've found an *old* letter,' insisted George, getting rather annoyed and scowling fiercely. Why did grown-ups always think children were being silly when they could be on the verge of an adventure?

'An *old* letter?' frowned Joanna, still looking rather dubious. 'And where might you have found such a thing?'

'In the cellar at Kirrin Farm!' said George, quickly showing it to her.

'Well, I never,' exclaimed the woman. 'I'd forgotten your grandad lived at Kirrin Farm years ago. My, my, Alf and his father *will* be pleased.'

'Yes,' said George, her eyes shining. 'I'm going to take it there right now!'

'Now, I don't think that's a very good idea,' said Joanna, shaking her head and putting the letter safely on the mantelpiece. 'As your grandfather wrote it, it really belongs to your mother now. You'd better ask her first.'

'But Joanna!' protested George. 'Alf's father is so worried. I'm sure Mummy will want him to know as quickly as possible.'

'That's as maybe,' said Joanna stubbornly. 'But you must still ask her first. Don't forget she's telephoning this evening. You can do it then.'

'Oh, blow, blow, blow!' said George, stamping her foot and going off in a huff. Why were grown-ups so jolly unreasonable? She gave a big sigh as she went up to her room. She had promised her mother she would do as Joanna said so there was nothing for it but to wait until this evening when she phoned.

But then she had a bright idea. 'I know,' she said to Timothy as she stomped up the stairs. 'I'll ask Father. It will be just as good as asking

71

Mummy. *He'll* let me take the letter to Alf, I know he will!'

But George's father was in the middle of a very important experiment and wouldn't come out when George knocked on his study door.

'Go away,' the stern man shouted. 'I'm very busy indeed!'

'But Father,' yelled George through the keyhole. 'I've found something very important and I need to talk to you!'

'I *said*, go away,' shouted her father. 'Whatever it is, it will just have to wait!'

George stamped her foot again. Why would *no-one* listen to her?

Timothy whined and licked the part of George's leg that was closest to his nose. He hated his little mistress being upset.

Still in a huff, the furious little girl stomped back down the stairs with Timothy at her heels. She went out into the garden, kicking at the stones on the path. She went to sit on her swing looking very fierce and moody. She thought of poor Alf and his father worrying themselves to death. She had wanted to help and now she had the chance, everyone was stopping her.

Timothy gave another little whine. He didn't know what had upset George but there had been a lot of shouting going on and he didn't like shouting one little bit.

But then suddenly George had a bright idea. She jumped off the swing, her eyes shining. 'I know, Timmy!' she cried. 'I don't care *what* Joanna or Father say. We'll go and tell Alf's father about the letter then give it to him tomorrow when we've spoken to Mummy. I know Mummy'll understand when she hears.

Come on, Timmy!' she added, running towards the gate. 'Hurry, hurry!'

Timothy rushed after her as fast as his short legs would carry him. He felt rather puzzled. One minute George was sulking, the next she was full of excitement and running towards the village although they had already been there once that day. *And* it was close to tea-time.

There was no doubt about it. Human beings were very strange creatures indeed!

8

Good news

It seemed like no time at all before the two were running excitedly across the beach towards the *Sally Ann*.

'Where are Alf and his father?' panted George to one of the fishermen.

'They're in the café,' said the man. 'They're trying to decide what to do if they lose their boat: the *Sally Ann*.'

'They're not going to lose her,' said George joyfully. 'I've found proof that she belongs to them.'

'Well, that *is* good news,' exclaimed the fisherman. 'You'd better go and tell them as fast as you can!'

George ran up the beach with Timothy and hurried across the road into the café.

The place was empty apart from Alf and his father and a man reading a newspaper. The man looked up and George gave him a broad grin as she went past. She felt so happy now that she had a smile for everyone. The man ignored her and went back to his newspaper.

Alf and his father were surprised to see George for the second time that day. Especially as she had such a happy look on her face. They both listened carefully as she blurted out her thrilling news.

'Yippee!' shouted Alf, giving Timothy such a big pat the puppy almost lost his balance. 'That's grand news, George!'

'Amongst your grandfather's papers in the

cellar at Kirrin Farm, eh?' said Alf's father, his wrinkly eyes lighting up. 'My word, that was a lucky find! Have you brought the letter with you?'

'I'm sorry,' said George, explaining. 'Joanna said the letter really belongs to Mummy and I've got to ask her first. But it's quite safe on the mantelpiece in the kitchen at Kirrin Cottage. Once I've spoken to Mummy I'll bring it straight to you and you can show it to that horrid ministry man.'

'He wasn't really that bad,' said Alf's father. 'He was just doing his job, that's all.'

The café doorbell clanged as the man who had been reading the newspaper left quickly. George glanced up and saw him hurrying off in the direction of the harbour. She chuckled to herself. He must have felt rather puzzled at all the excitement going on.

'Thanks, George,' said Alf, patting her on the back. 'You're a really good friend.'

'Well, it looks as though our troubles are over,' said his father, his face wrinkling again as he smiled. 'You're a real hero, Master George!'

Alf and his father bought George and Timothy an ice-cream to celebrate. George had a choc ice and Timothy a cornet. He licked the ice-cream as fast as he could before it melted.

'Good old, Timmy,' laughed Alf, watching as the puppy crunched up the cornet then licked the ice-cream from around his whiskery mouth with his big, pink tongue. 'If it hadn't been for him chasing that rat you would never have found the letter.'

'I know,' said George, hugging Timothy. 'He's the real hero, not me!'

After tea, George waited impatiently for her mother to ring. Father had been so busy he hadn't even come out of his study for the omelette that Joanna had promised him. In fact no-one had seen him since breakfast time.

George was quite pleased her father hadn't appeared. If he had seen Timothy lying under the tea table he might have remembered he had banished him!

When at last the telephone did ring, George hurried to answer it. Her mother listened carefully to the story of their adventure.

'That's wonderful news, darling,' she exclaimed. 'Fancy you finding a letter written by my father all those years ago. We must have left all those things in the cellar when we moved from Kirrin Farm to the cottage.'

'So is it all right to give it to Alf's father?' George asked anxiously.

'Yes, of course it is, dear,' said her mother. 'Take it to them first thing in the morning!'

'I will,' said George. 'Thanks, Mummy. I knew you wouldn't mind but Joanna said I must ask you first.'

'Yes, she was quite right,' said her mother.

'Are you having a nice time in London?' enquired George, suddenly remembering she hadn't asked.

'Yes, lovely,' said her mother. 'Your noisy cousins have gone away so it's very nice and quiet, except for the traffic, of course.'

'How awful,' said George screwing up her nose. 'I'm jolly glad I stayed at home!'

George could hardly sleep that night, she felt so full of excitement. Timothy wasn't really allowed to sleep in her room but as usual she crept down the stairs to fetch him after she had heard her father go to bed. She could never bear to think of the puppy all alone in the big kitchen. Each morning before her parents were awake, she would take him back down again so no-one would know he had been there.

Luckily, no-one ever asked where the puppy had slept so George didn't have to confess the truth. She never told lies and would have had to tell her parents if they had asked.

It was a bright moonlit night as George sat on the bed with Timothy. They both gazed out of the window. She could see the twinkling lights of the fishing vessels far out to sea.

'Now Alf and his father won't have to worry any more, will they, Timmy?' said the little girl, giving the puppy a happy hug. 'I simply can't wait to give them the letter.'

Timothy gave a little whine then turned round and round to make himself a nest on George's bed. He lay down and gave a big sigh. In no time at all he was fast asleep, one ear cocked for danger as usual.

George crawled under the covers and settled down. She felt sleepy now too. It had been such an exciting day!

It was gone midnight when Timothy suddenly awoke. He lifted his head, both ears pricked. There was a strange noise coming from downstairs. A scraping, scrabbling sound, then a dull thud.

Timothy cocked his head to one side. What on earth was it? Surely there weren't any rats at Kirrin Cottage?

Beside him, his little mistress was fast asleep. Timothy jumped off the bed and padded to the door, still listening intently. There were soft footsteps moving about downstairs. Had George's father got up for a drink of water? Timothy gave a little whine. He had heard Father's footsteps before. He often got up to go to his study in the middle of the night. But these footsteps were different altogether. They were the soft, wary footsteps of a stranger!

Timothy gave a sudden bark and began to scrabble at the door.

George woke up straight away, sitting up and rubbing her eyes. She glanced at the clock beside the bed. It was one o'clock in the morning.

'Ssh, Timmy, you'll wake Father and he'll know you're up here,' she whispered.

But Timmy went on scratching frantically at the door.

George threw back the covers, got out of bed

and tip-toed over to him. 'What's wrong?' she whispered. 'Do you want to go out?'

Timmy whined and scrabbled some more. He simply had to go downstairs and investigate the strange noise at once!

'All right,' whispered George. 'But don't let Father hear you!' She opened the door and the little dog hurtled down the stairs, barking madly.

'Oh, blow!' exclaimed George to herself, running after him on the tips of her bare toes. 'Father's bound to wake up. Now we'll *both* be in trouble!'

Timothy was standing outside the kitchen door, barking and whining and scratching frantically to try to get in.

'What is it, Tim? What's wrong?' whispered George, her heart thudding. Then she heard the strange noises too. A thump and a clatter. Someone was moving around in the kitchen. Maybe it was her father, fetching a drink of water? But all the upstairs doors had been closed as she slipped past. The kitchen door was closed too. If Father had been getting a drink he wouldn't bother to close all the doors behind him.

George froze, her heart beating like a drum. There was an intruder in Kirrin Cottage!

9

Stolen!

Timothy was making such a row that he woke George's father. His bedroom door burst open and he stormed out on to the landing.

'What's all the noise about?' came his furious voice from the top of the stairs. His dark brows were drawn together in a frown. 'How on earth am I expected to sleep with this racket going on?'

George ran up the stairs. 'Father, there's someone in the kitchen,' she whispered fiercely. 'Timmy heard them!' She completely forgot that the puppy was supposed to be asleep in the kitchen. Luckily, her father was too concerned to notice.

'In the kitchen?' he frowned. 'What? Do you mean an intruder?'

'Yes,' whispered George trying not to feel scared. 'It must be. Timmy's going mad.'

'I can hear him!' said her father, pushing past her to get to the bottom of the stairs. 'Out of my way, dog. Let's have a look!' he said, grabbing a walking stick from the hall stand.

'Be careful, Father,' called George as he threw open the kitchen door and clicked on the light.

Timothy hurtled in, almost tripping Father up as he stood on the threshold brandishing the walking stick. 'Who's there?' he shouted angrily. 'Show yourself, I order you!'

But to their surprise, the kitchen was empty. George peeped round her father and saw that the floor was scattered with bills and papers that had fallen off the mantelpiece. Some

ornaments and photographs had been tossed on to the floor. The window was wide open and there were dirty boot marks on the sill.

Someone had been snooping around but had escaped through the open window!

Timothy ran around the room, sniffing. His tail was bolt upright, waving like a banner. His heart thudded nineteen to the dozen. There was a strange smell in here. A strong, salty kind of smell. It was all around the room. He jumped up at the window, yelping and trying to see out.

'I say, the window catch has been forced,' said George's father, going over to take a closer look. 'This is where the scoundrel got in *and* out.'

'But why would anyone want to break into our kitchen?' asked George in a puzzled voice. She gave a shiver to think someone had been poking around downstairs when they were all asleep. 'Surely no-one would want to steal pots and pans?'

'I wouldn't think so,' said her father, looking very puzzled. 'They were probably hoping to search in the other rooms but Timothy disturbed them. I'd better telephone PC Moon and tell him we've had an intruder.' He went out into the hall to use the telephone.

Timothy was still running around sniffing. He felt most annoyed that the intruder had escaped. He would have loved to have bitten him hard or at least torn a piece off his trousers. He whined at the back door to go out. He could probably follow the man's scent and find out which way he went.

George opened the door and the puppy hurtled out. The salty smell was stronger than ever out here. He ran around the garden shed. The smell was very strong and the door was ajar. The puppy peered inside. A dark, menacing figure was crouched by the wheelbarrow.

The intruder hadn't gone at all. He was hiding in the garden shed!

Timothy gave another, triumphant bark and charged in.

Indoors, George was picking up all the papers that were scattered everywhere. She felt quite shaky and couldn't get over feeling scared that a stranger had been snooping around inside Kirrin Cottage. Her mother would be terribly upset.

She heard her father speaking on the phone in the hall as she stood on a chair to put the things back on the mantelpiece.

'PC Moon says we must check if anything is missing,' said George's father coming back into the room. 'He'll come round in the morning to take a statement.'

George was just about to reply when a loud barking came from outside, followed by the sound of a man shouting.

'Timmy!' cried George in horror, suddenly realising the puppy was still out in the garden. 'It sounds as if he's found something!'

'You stay here, George. I'll see to it,' said her father rushing outside before she had time to argue. He was just in time to see the burly shadow of a man dashing through the orchard with Timothy in hot pursuit. Timothy had flushed him out of the shed and the man was trying to dodge the angry puppy and make his escape before he was discovered.

George's father had almost caught up with

him when the intruder vaulted the hedge at the bottom of the garden. There was a loud thud as he fell. Cursing loudly he scrambled to his feet and ran off. Father rushed to the gate and shouted for him to stop. But he had gone, running down the path then crashing through the heather until the sounds died away.

Timothy was charging up and down the side of the hedge but couldn't push his way through. He stood at the gate, barking furiously. If only he was a grown-up dog he

could have jumped the hedge and run after the horrid man!

When the little dog saw the man had escaped he picked something up off the ground and ran back to George waiting at the kitchen door. He put it down proudly at her feet. It wasn't *quite* as good as a rat but a lot better than nothing at all.

'What's this?' said his mistress, bending to pick it up. 'Oh, Father, look, it's a piece of someone's trousers!' Her father had come back to the house looking very angry indeed. She handed him a ragged piece of thick, blue material. 'Good boy, Timmy!' she cried bending to hug him. 'He must have ripped it off the burglar's trousers. Isn't he brave, Father?'

'Jolly brave,' said her father, bending to give Timothy a pat. 'But unfortunately not big enough to stop the scoundrel getting away. I wish I'd been with him, I would have sorted the villain out!'

'Me too!' said George.

'Come on, George, let's get back indoors and see if anything is missing,' said her father, putting his arm round her and taking her back inside. Timothy followed, still feeling angry that the intruder had got away. Still, he had taken a good bite out of his trousers and it jolly well served him right!

'Well, I can't see anything is missing,' said George's father when they had taken a good look round the kitchen and put the rest of the things back.

'Perhaps he was a hungry tramp after something to eat?' suggested George.

'But nothing has gone from the larder,' said Father, frowning deeply. 'It really is rather a riddle.'

'Well, then . . .' began George but stopped suddenly as a feeling of horror crept over her. She'd had a sudden, frightening thought. She clambered up on the chair and got the pile of letters and papers down again. She searched through them frantically, her heart sinking right down to her feet.

'What on earth are you doing, George?' frowned her father. 'We've only just put all those back.'

'Oh, Father,' cried George, trying her best not to cry. She thought crying was weak and babyish but this time she could hardly stop a tear rolling down her cheek. Her worst fear had come true. 'Grandfather's letter! It's gone!'

10

A clue

'Letter?' exclaimed George's father looking puzzled. 'What letter?' He had been too busy to listen to George earlier when she came to tell him about her find in the cellar at Kirrin Farm, so didn't know *what* she was talking about.

George explained tearfully.

'And you say there were lots of papers in the trunk?' said her father when she told him what she had found.

'Yes,' confirmed George. 'A whole bundle of them but I only brought one envelope home. I first noticed it because it had an unusual stamp on it and I thought you might like to see it.'

'Mmm,' said her father stroking his chin and looking thoughtful. 'The others might have been important too, you know, George.'

'Well *this* one was the most important,' insisted George. 'I didn't care about the others. I just wanted to help Alf and his father and now I can't.' She stamped her foot angrily, forgetting her tears. 'It's simply too rotten!'

'And that rascal has stolen it,' said her father, still looking thoughtful. 'How did he know it was here?'

'I've no idea,' said George, racking her brains for who could have possibly known about the letter. 'There's only me and Timmy, Mummy and Alf – and his father, of course.'

'But why would anyone want to steal it?' said her father. 'What would be the point?'

George gave an irritated sigh. Her father was a very clever scientist but sometimes he couldn't work out the most simple problem. 'To stop Alf and his father proving they own the *Sally Ann*, of course!' she said. 'What other reason could there possibly be?'

'Well, I don't know who would do such a thing,' said Father, stroking his chin in a very puzzled manner and shaking his head. 'No-one in Kirrin would act in such a cowardly way.'

George's father put his arm around her and lead her out of the kitchen. 'I'm afraid there's nothing more we can do. The letter's gone and that's that. Come on, George, you'd better get back to bed. Mummy won't be very pleased if you look tired when she gets back from London.'

George was so upset as she trailed up the stairs that she didn't even remember to leave Timothy in the kitchen. Luckily, her father was upset too, and didn't notice the puppy had followed them up and slipped into her room.

'Goodnight, George,' said her father kindly as he went off to his own room. Although he often quarrelled with his fierce little daughter he loved her very much and didn't like to see her upset.

'Goodnight, Father,' said George miserably.

Joanna was shocked to see the broken window catch when she came to work the following morning.

'A burglar?' exclaimed the poor woman, looking upset. 'Oh, dearie, me! He could have got away with your father's important papers from his study!'

'No, he couldn't,' said George. 'Timothy frightened him away.'

'Well, it still leaves me with a horrible feeling,' said Joanna angrily. 'I'd like to have got my hands on him!'

'Timmy got his teeth into him,' said George showing her the ragged material Timothy had torn from the burglar's trouser leg.

'It looks like a piece from a pair of sailor's trousers,' said Joanna gazing at it thoughtfully. 'But there aren't any sailors in Kirrin. I wonder who it could have been?'

'I don't know,' replied George pulling a face. 'I only wish I did!'

George and Timothy went outside. George knew she would soon have to go and tell Alf and his father the bad news. It was no good putting it off. It simply had to be done.

A car drew up outside and PC Moon got out. He had come to take a statement. 'I'll take that piece of cloth as evidence,' said the policeman when George and her father had told him everything. 'Well done!' he said to Timothy. 'You'd make a good police-dog when you grow up.'

'No, he wouldn't,' argued George, hugging Timothy. 'He's going to be my dog for ever.'

Timothy wagged his tail. He very much liked being praised. Especially by this man who looked rather important in his dark uniform with the shiny buttons.

'Come on, Tim,' said George with a sigh when the policeman had gone. 'We'd better go and see Alf.'

George went down the path towards the gate, feeling very unhappy indeed. This was going to be the most terrible thing she had ever had to do.

Timothy bounded on ahead, waiting by the gate for George to open it. Once through, he stopped and sniffed the air. That strange, salty scent he had smelled last night was still here.

Suddenly, with his nose to the ground, the puppy shot off. The salty smell led away from the village path down towards the beach. He was quite determined to follow it.

'Hey, Timmy!' called George. 'You're going the wrong way!'

Timothy was usually very obedient but this time he simply wouldn't come back, however loudly George shouted. He shot down the narrow path that led to the beach, his plumy tail waving like a banner. Sniff, sniff, he went like a bloodhound on the trail.

'Timmy!' yelled George, running after him. 'Come back!'

All the way down to the cove they went, the puppy running as fast as he could with George panting along behind him. She was very annoyed with him. It was most unlike him to run off without her.

When Timothy reached the shore, he ran round and round in circles. For a moment or two he lost the scent. Then he picked it up again and ran up and down the beach, barking and barking.

'Timmy!' scolded George, when at last she caught up with him. 'What *has* got into you? What can you smell?'

Then she saw what the puppy had been sniffing. There in the sand were the deep grooves of a rowing boat. The only boat that ever came to Kirrin Bay was George's own small dinghy which was still safely moored closer to the house. These deep grooves had been made by a strange, heavy boat.

There was something else too. Large footprints above the high water mark close to where the boat had been dragged up on the sand.

George frowned as she crouched down to examine them. Timothy still ran round excitedly, sniffing and sniffing.

George looked up at him, her eyes shining excitedly. 'This boat has been pulled up high out of the way of the tide,' she exclaimed. 'So it must have been here very, very early this morning.'

'Wuff,' said Timothy sitting down beside her and smiling, his big pink tongue lolling out.

'Oh, Timmy,' exclaimed George excitedly. 'I bet whoever it was who broke into the house last night came in a boat! We didn't hear a car or anything and he ran out of the garden and down to the bay. No *wonder* he got away!'

11

Back to the farm

'Come on, Timmy,' said George when she had finished examining the grooves in the sand. 'Let's get back and tell Father what we've found!'

'Wuff,' agreed Timothy, running beside her. This was a very exciting start to the day!

'Father! Father!' called George as she ran

indoors, quite forgetting he might be angry at being disturbed.

'He's just gone to the village to post some important letters,' said Joanna as George hurtled in through the back door with Timothy at her heels.

'We'll probably meet him on his way back, then,' said George skidding to a halt. 'We can tell him then. Come on, Timmy, let's go and find Alf.'

Half way along the garden path George suddenly stopped. Father had gone to post some important letters, Joanna had said. George remembered her conversation with her father the previous night. Something about there being other important letters in that old trunk in the cellar. Supposing another one of them was about the *Sally Ann?*

Timothy was staring up at her, wondering why she had suddenly stopped dead on the path.

'Timmy!' she said excitedly. 'I've just had an idea. Let's go back to the farm and search through that old trunk. Maybe we shan't have to tell Alf and his father any bad news after all!' She ran to the gate, her heart suddenly full of excitement. Timothy ran after her, feeling rather surprised at this sudden change of plan. He had heard the word 'village' and thought they were going there. Now they were off to the farm again. What on earth was going on?

As they went through the gate his nose caught that salty smell again. He sniffed around the hedge. It was here, stronger than ever.

'Buck up!' shouted George, way ahead already. 'We've got something very important to do today, Timmy. No hanging about!'

Timothy gave up sniffing the smell and ran after her. He decided he would look again later when they came back.

It was another warm, sunny day although there were some dark clouds out to sea and it looked as if the weather might break later on. As they took the route across the common, George could see the gulls circling around Kirrin Island and tiny waves breaking on the shore.

She hurried on. They were on a very serious mission and there was no time to stand and stare.

By now the puppy was looking forward to seeing his new friends again. If he felt very brave he might even go and bark at that big bull!

As the two hurried into the farm yard George saw there was a big, beefy-looking man dressed in dark trousers and a navy blue jumper at the front door. He was talking to Mrs Sanders in a very loud voice that echoed across the yard. There was no sign of old Mr Sanders or the farm dogs.

Timothy gave a low growl and stopped in his tracks. He didn't like the look of the stranger one little bit. Even from this distance he could tell he wasn't very nice. He was looming over the old woman with one elbow propped against the door frame.

'It's all right, Timmy,' said George. 'He's probably a friend of the Sanders.'

But Timothy wouldn't budge. He planted his four paws firmly on the ground and stared at the visitor, the fur on the back of his neck standing on end. He could tell whether a human was friendly or not and this one definitely wasn't.

'Timothy,' began George sternly. 'Come on, please!'

Suddenly there was a small cry from Mrs Sanders and the man began shouting at her. The old lady put her hand over her mouth and shook her head. 'No, no, I tell you, I know nothing about a letter.'

'Oh yes you do, you silly old woman,' shouted the man. 'Now don't tell me lies!'

'I'm *not*,' insisted Mrs Sanders in a shaky voice. 'I don't know what you're talking about. I don't know anything about any letters.'

George suddenly understood why Timothy hadn't wanted to go into the yard. The puppy was very good at sensing danger.

'Let's go and hide behind the barn,' whispered George. 'We can spy on him from there.'

So the two crept through the gate and round behind the barn where they could spy on the

stranger. George crouched down with her hand on Timothy's collar.

'My husband will be back any minute,' she heard Mrs Sanders say bravely. 'So you had better get going.'

'Not until I've looked through that old trunk,' said the man. 'Now where is it?' He turned a little sideways so George could see the side of his face.

Hidden by the barn, George gave a gasp of horror. She recognised the man at once. He had been sitting in the café when she was telling Alf and his father about the letter. He must have overheard them.

'Timmy!' hissed the little girl. 'I bet he's the one who broke in last night and pinched that letter!'

'Wuff,' said Timothy sniffing the air, his tail standing right up on end. He could smell that salty smell again. The same smell that was in the kitchen, *and* all around the garden. The clever little dog already knew it was the man who had stolen the letter. He quivered. If only his mistress would let go of his collar he

111

would run and bite the man's leg. He wouldn't be content with just tearing his trousers this time!

'But why is he here threatening Mrs Sanders?' whispered George, feeling rather puzzled. 'If he's already got the letter, why does he want to see if there are any others?'

'Wuff,' said Timothy softly.

'Stay!' hissed George when she felt Timothy quivering. 'It's no good you rushing over there. We've got to think of a plan!'

'Grrr,' said Timothy. 'Wuff!' He already had a good plan. Biting legs was the best plan in the world!

Then George suddenly had a bright idea. An idea that, if it worked, would scare the awful man away for good!

'Come on, Tim,' she hissed, creeping away. 'Follow me!'

Timothy took one last look at the man. He was still shouting at Mrs Sanders. The old lady looked very scared but she was still refusing to let him into the house. Any minute now the villain might push past her and barge his way in. There was no time to lose.

Keeping low and making themselves as small as they could, the two crept round to the back of the barn.

'Here we are,' said George as they reached Billy the bull in his pen. The great creature stared at her and blinked his big eyes as if he wondered where on earth this small girl and dog had appeared from.

Timothy stood and watched as George

climbed up the side of the pen. The little dog felt rather puzzled. What on earth was his mistress up to *now*?

12

Out of luck

'I'm just undoing the catch,' panted George as she climbed up the bars and tried her best to slide the big bolt across to undo the bull's pen. 'When I've done it, I want you to go behind and bark and bark so that Billy comes out. He'll run straight into the yard and scare that horrid man away for good.'

'Wurf,' said Timothy. This was a rather hair-brained scheme of George's but he had a sneaking feeling that it might just work.

Billy the bull looked up in surprise as George managed to slide the heavy bolt across and the gate swung open on its huge hinges. George scrambled sideways to the back of the pen and gave him a big slap on the back. 'Go on, Billy, out you go!'

'Wuff, wuff!' went Timothy as loudly as he could, glad to be able to give a jolly good bark at last. Dodging the animal's huge feet, he scampered to the back of the pen. 'Wuff, wuff,' he barked as the great beast went lumbering out.

George jumped down and ran after him. She picked up a stick and gave him a gentle tap on his rear end. 'Go, Billy!' she shouted. 'Go!'

The bull shook his great head and lumbered on round the side of the barn. He could see the farmer's wife at the door of the farmhouse. She was a kind woman and often brought him tit-bits. Maybe she would have one for him now?

George suddenly gave a shout. 'Help! Help!'

yelled the little girl at the top of her voice. 'The bull's out! Mrs Sanders, mind out of the way, quick!'

'Wuff, wuff!' barked Timothy. He suddenly realised what George was up to.

Into the yard lumbered the great beast, snorting and tossing his head. It was good to stretch his legs after being penned up. He began to run towards the house, his long tail swishing, his head tossing and his great horns flashing in the sunlight.

The man turned in horror when he heard hooves clip-clopping across the yard. His mouth fell open and all the blood drained from his face as Billy came lumbering straight towards him.

Mrs Sanders had heard George shout and spotted her and Timothy lurking round the side of the barn watching Billy. She realised what they were doing at once.

'Oh goodness!' cried the old lady in her loudest voice. 'You'd better get out of the way. That animal's extremely dangerous!'

But the scoundrel didn't need to be told. He

took one petrified glance at the great animal trotting towards him and fled for his life. He sped across the yard and through the gate, disappearing down the lane as fast as his legs would carry him.

By now, Billy had changed direction. He had spotted the cows looking over the gate with great interest at the goings on. He turned and trotted towards them giving a great, echoing bellow that must have reached the fleeing man and scared him even more.

'Oh, Master George!' cried Mrs Sanders. 'I *am* pleased to see you!'

'Are you all right?' asked George anxiously. 'We heard that horrible man shouting at you.'

'Yes, yes. I'm fine. I don't know who he was but I was very scared. Thank you so much, you're a very brave little girl.'

'Timmy's brave too,' said George. 'He knew that man was being horrible to you.'

'Good boy!' exclaimed the old lady, bending to give Timothy a pat. 'Come on, let's put old Billy back into his pen.'

George and Timothy helped Mrs Sanders lead

the bull back into his pen. He lumbered in willingly, quite tired from all the excitement. Mrs Sanders went to pull a fistful of fresh grass from the field and Billy chomped away gratefully as George climbed up the bars and patted his great neck. 'Well done, Billy,' she said, laughing. 'Didn't that man look funny running away?'

'He certainly did,' said Mrs Sanders, laughing so much her eyes were running. 'And old Billy wouldn't hurt a fly!'

'Wuff,' said Timothy rushing to sniff the man's scent where he had stood on the doorstep. 'Wurf, wurf!'

Mrs Sanders took the two indoors for some lemonade and biscuits. 'I still don't have any idea what he wanted,' she said, bustling around in the kitchen. 'He was on about letters or something.'

'I know what he meant,' said George and proceeded to tell Mrs Sanders the whole story.

'Well, I never,' said the old lady, looking very surprised indeed. 'I had no idea there were any old letters in the cellar.'

'But what *I* don't understand,' added George, 'is why he wanted to look for *more* letters when he's already stolen the most important one?'

'I've no idea,' said Mrs Sanders looking just as puzzled as George.

'Please could I go back down to the cellar and find that old trunk again?' asked George when she had finished her lemonade. 'I'm dying to see if there are any more papers that might help my friend Alf.'

'Help yourself,' said Mrs Sanders. 'And I hope you have some luck, my dear.'

So George and Timothy went back down into the old, musty cellar. This time, George was careful to fix the trap-door back before she climbed down. Mr Sanders had oiled the hinges and it opened easily this time.

She soon found the old trunk and hauled out the letters. She took them over to the hatch where the light shone down into the cellar and she could read them.

'There's no more here about the *Sally Ann*,' she sighed sitting cross-legged on the floor with

Timothy beside her. A bundle of envelopes lay in her lap. 'They're only old bills and papers. It looks as if we're out of luck, Timmy.'

'Wurf,' said Timothy softly. He knew his mistress was sad and wished there was something he could do.

At last George got to her feet. She tipped all the papers back into the trunk and closed the lid. 'Come on, Tim. It looks as if we've got to go and see Alf and his father after all.'

George said goodbye and set off home feeling

very sad. It looked as if the battle to save the *Sally Ann* had been lost for ever.

When they reached the gate of Kirrin Cottage, Timothy suddenly shot off along the hedge. George was too unhappy to be bothered to call him back so she went into the garden leaving the gate open for him to follow. She knew Timothy wouldn't stay away from her for long.

'Where have you been all morning?' asked Joanna as George went into the kitchen. She was getting lunch ready for George and her father, and could tell by the little girl's face that she wasn't at all happy.

George explained, then perched herself up on the kitchen table swinging her legs to and fro in her usual manner. 'I didn't find any more letters but we *did* find the burglar.'

'The burglar,' exclaimed Joanna. 'Don't be silly, George. How could you have found the burglar?'

'Well we did,' insisted George, telling Joanna what had happened.

'You'd better ask your father to telephone PC

Moon,' said the housekeeper. 'He'll be very interested, I'm sure.'

'Yes, I suppose so,' sighed George. 'Although we don't know who he was so I don't see that it'll make any difference.'

'Well you can give him a description,' said Joanna.

'Very well,' sighed George. 'Is Father in his study?'

'No,' said Joanna, shaking her head. 'He's out in the . . .'

But a sudden shout from outside interrupted her. It was George's father and he sounded very angry. 'Timothy, come here *at once* and show me what you've got hold of now!'

13

Timmy saves the day

Father had been sitting under the apple tree reading his scientific magazine and had spotted Timothy hurtling past with something in his mouth.

George's father followed the puppy indoors looking rather angry and red in the face. 'Drop!' he shouted at Timothy. 'Drop, at once!'

'Don't shout, Father,' said George getting down from the table. 'You know Timmy hates being yelled at. Leave!' she said firmly to the puppy. 'Leave!'

Timothy sat down and dropped the article at her feet.

'Thank you,' said George. 'Good boy! There you are, Father, you only have to ask!'

Timothy sat looking up at her, his tongue hanging out and his smiley eyes gleaming. He knew she would be pleased with her gift.

George's father wasn't listening. He had picked up the article and was gazing at it with a puzzled frown on his face. It was a rather damp and muddy envelope. 'I thought it might be a letter I may have dropped on my way to the post office yesterday but it isn't,' he exclaimed.

'Oh!' cried George, hardly able to believe her eyes. 'Father! It's *my* letter. The one I found at the farm.' She took it from her father's fingers, her blue eyes shining with joy. 'Timmy! Where was it?'

'Wuff,' said Timothy, running to and fro from

the back door. He wanted to show George where he had found it.

But George had already guessed. 'I bet that's what he smelled under the hedge. He was rushing about out there like mad!' cried George. 'Oh, Timmy! You're the cleverest dog in the whole world!' She bent to give him such a big hug the little dog could hardly breathe. Timothy wagged his tail so hard it looked as if it might fall off!

'Well, I never,' said Joanna staring at the envelope. 'Whatever next? Come on, Timmy, I'll find you a special bone for being so clever.'

'Wuff,' said Timothy joyfully, trotting after her as she went into the pantry. The best reward of all was a juicy bone. He clamped his jaws around it and took it out into the garden to chew.

'That explains why that horrid man was at the farm,' said George to her father. 'He must have dropped the letter when he jumped over our hedge and he wanted to see if there were any more like it.'

'What man?' said Father, frowning. 'Honestly George, sometimes you do talk in riddles.'

Just as she was about to explain, Joanna called to them from the kitchen. 'Lunch is ready!'

So George told her father about their adventure at the farm over a delicious lunch of crispy salad and hard boiled eggs with homemade bread rolls straight from the oven, followed by a slice of one of Joanna's sugary apple pies which George simply *had* to gobble up before she finished the story.

Father smiled when he heard what had happened with Billy the bull. 'I don't know,' he said feeling rather proud of his small daughter, 'you really are a little tomboy, you know. All these scrapes you get into!'

'Oh, thank you, Father,' cried the little girl, grinning from ear to ear. 'That's the very best thing you've ever said to me!'

'What is?' came a voice from the doorway. They turned to see George's mother, home from her visit to London. She had missed them so much that she had decided to come back early.

So George had to tell the tale all over again.

'I don't like the sound of that man,' said her mother worriedly when she heard about the burglar. 'You'd better ring PC Moon again, Quentin, and tell him he went to the farm.'

'Very well,' said her husband getting up from the lunch table. 'Then I really must get on with my work. There have been far too many interruptions today!'

'Mummy,' said George excitedly, getting down from the table. 'Timmy and I have got to go down to the harbour and give the letter to

Alf's father straight away. He must be wondering why we haven't turned up before.'

She rushed outside where she found Timothy digging a hole to bury his bone.

'Timmy!' she scolded, hurrying to fill in the hole which was right in the middle of her mother's flower bed.

Timothy whined as she picked up the rather muddy bone and put it in the garden shed. 'You can have it as soon as we get back,' she promised.

George put the letter carefully into the pocket of her shorts as the two hurried to the village. She simply couldn't wait to give Alf the letter.

They found the boy and his father unloading their day's catch from the *Sally Ann*. They had sailed in with the tide and the boxes of fresh fish were stacked up along the harbour wall.

Alf was just unloading the last one as George and Timothy hurried across the beach towards them.

'We've got it,' cried the little girl taking the letter from her pocket and waving it at him. 'We've got the letter!'

Alf's father overheard and came running down the gang-plank. 'Master George!' cried the fisherman, his weathered face lighting up. 'We've been wondering where you'd got to!'

'It's a long story,' said George handing her grandfather's letter to the grateful man and jumping up and down with excitement. 'Open it, then. Open it!'

'Well, this is all we need,' said the fisherman as he read the letter. 'It means we can keep the *Sally Ann*.' He looked at George and she thought she could see a tear twinkling in his eye. 'I don't know how to thank you, George.'

'Let's have a look, Dad,' said Alf, anxious to read the good news for himself. His face lit up when he read it. 'Gosh, thanks, George,' he said, grinning from ear to ear. 'You've been jolly brave and clever.'

'And Timmy,' said George. 'He's been brave and clever too. If it hadn't been for him the letter might have been lost for ever.'

'Lost?' asked Alf curiously, so she had to quickly tell them the whole story all over again.

Alf's father frowned when she described the

burglar. 'And he was wearing dark blue sailor's trousers,' said George. 'Timothy ripped a bit out of them.'

'Sailor's trousers, eh?' said the burly fisherman thoughtfully. 'That sounds like Bert Crump to me. He was in the navy years ago.'

'Isn't he the man from the next village who wants to move to Kirrin and fish the waters?' exclaimed Alf with a frown.

'That's right,' said his father. 'But he hasn't been able to get a licence *and* he was in the café that day when George told us about the letter. He's got a rowing boat he moors up by the harbour wall.'

'I *knew* it was the same man,' cried George excitedly. 'I recognised him the moment I saw him.'

'Aye,' said the fisherman. 'He's known to be a bit of a rogue. I wouldn't put it past him to write to the Ministry and tell lies about the *Sally Ann*. I don't know why I haven't thought of him before.'

'But why would he do such a horrid thing?' asked George, puzzled.

'Because my father's a very good fisherman and he's jealous,' said Alf angrily. 'And if we were banned from fishing it would mean there would be space for one more in the fleet.'

'And that one more could be Bert,' finished his father. 'You know, George, I'm sure PC Moon would like to hear all this.'

'My father's going to ring him and tell him,' said George.

'If the police search his house and find the torn trousers then that will be enough to prove his guilt,' said Alf. 'He'll be in court for breaking and entering Kirrin Cottage in no time at all.'

'Jolly good,' said George feeling rather satisfied. Whatever happened, she didn't think Bert Crump would be bothering Alf and his father again.

'Thanks, you two,' called Alf again, waving as George and Timothy set off home. 'Thanks for everything!'

George waved back as she climbed up the cliff path on her way back to Kirrin Cottage. Overhead the gulls whirled and the purple heathers nodded their pretty heads at her as she passed. Timothy ran on ahead, diving after a white bob-tail that disappeared into the bushes.

'Buck up, Timmy,' called George as he began to get left behind. 'We'll go down to the beach this afternoon if you like, now our adventure is over and the *Sally Ann's* saved.'

'Wuff!' barked the puppy as he caught up with her. Playing on the sand was another of his very favourite things. In fact, when he thought about it, *everything* he did with George was his favourite thing.

The little girl stuck her hands in her pockets and whistled a jolly tune as she strode along. 'That was a really thrilling adventure, don't you think, Timmy?' she said, chuckling when she thought about Bert Crump running away from dear old gentle Billy.

'Wurf,' agreed Timothy scampering on ahead.

George was quite right, he thought. It had been a very, very exciting adventure indeed!

Just George 5:
George, Timmy and the Stranger in the Storm

Sue Welford

George and Timmy are watching a storm from an upstairs window at Kirrin Cottage when a flash of lightning reveals a small figure running along the cliff path. The next day they discover a boy sheltering nearby. He's on the run from cruel carers and begs George not to tell anyone he's there. So, when a strange couple turn up asking questions, George decides it's time to find him a new hiding place . . .

Another Hodder Children's book

Just George 6:
George, Timmy and the Lighthouse
Mystery

Sue Welford

George has spotted an escaped convict in
Kirrin Village. She recognises his picture
from the local paper. But why is he hanging
around the boarded-up old lighthouse?
George and Timmy don't have a clue – until
they overhear a secret conversation about
a hoard of stolen jewels . . .

ORDER FORM

Just George

Sue Welford

0 340 77863 6	1: George, Timmy and the Haunted Cave	£3.50	❐
0 340 77864 4	2: George, Timmy and the Curious Treasure	£3.50	❐
0 340 77871 7	3: George, Timmy and the Footprint in the Sand	£3.50	❐
0 340 77876 8	4: George, Timmy and the Secret in the Cellar	£3.50	❐
0 340 77879 2	5: George, Timmy and the Stranger in the Storm	£3.50	❐
0 340 77882 2	6: George, Timmy and the Lighthouse Mystery	£3.50	❐

All Hodder Children's books are available at your local bookshop, or can be ordered direct from the publisher. Just tick the titles you would like and complete the details below. Prices and availability are subject to change without prior notice.

Please enclose a cheque or postal order made payable to *Bookpoint Ltd*, and send to: Hodder Children's Books, 39 Milton Park, Abingdon, OXON OX14 4TD, UK.
Email Address: orders@bookpoint.co.uk

If you would prefer to pay by credit card, our call centre team would be delighted to take your order by telephone. Our direct line *01235 400414* (lines open 9.00 am–6.00 pm Monday to Saturday, 24 hour message answering service). Alternatively you can send a fax on *01235 400454*.

TITLE		FIRST NAME		SURNAME	

ADDRESS	
DAYTIME TEL:	POST CODE

If you would prefer to pay by credit card, please complete:
Please debit my Visa/Access/Diner's Card/American Express (delete as applicable) card no:

Signature .... Expiry Date: ....

If you would NOT like to receive further information on our products please tick the box. ❐